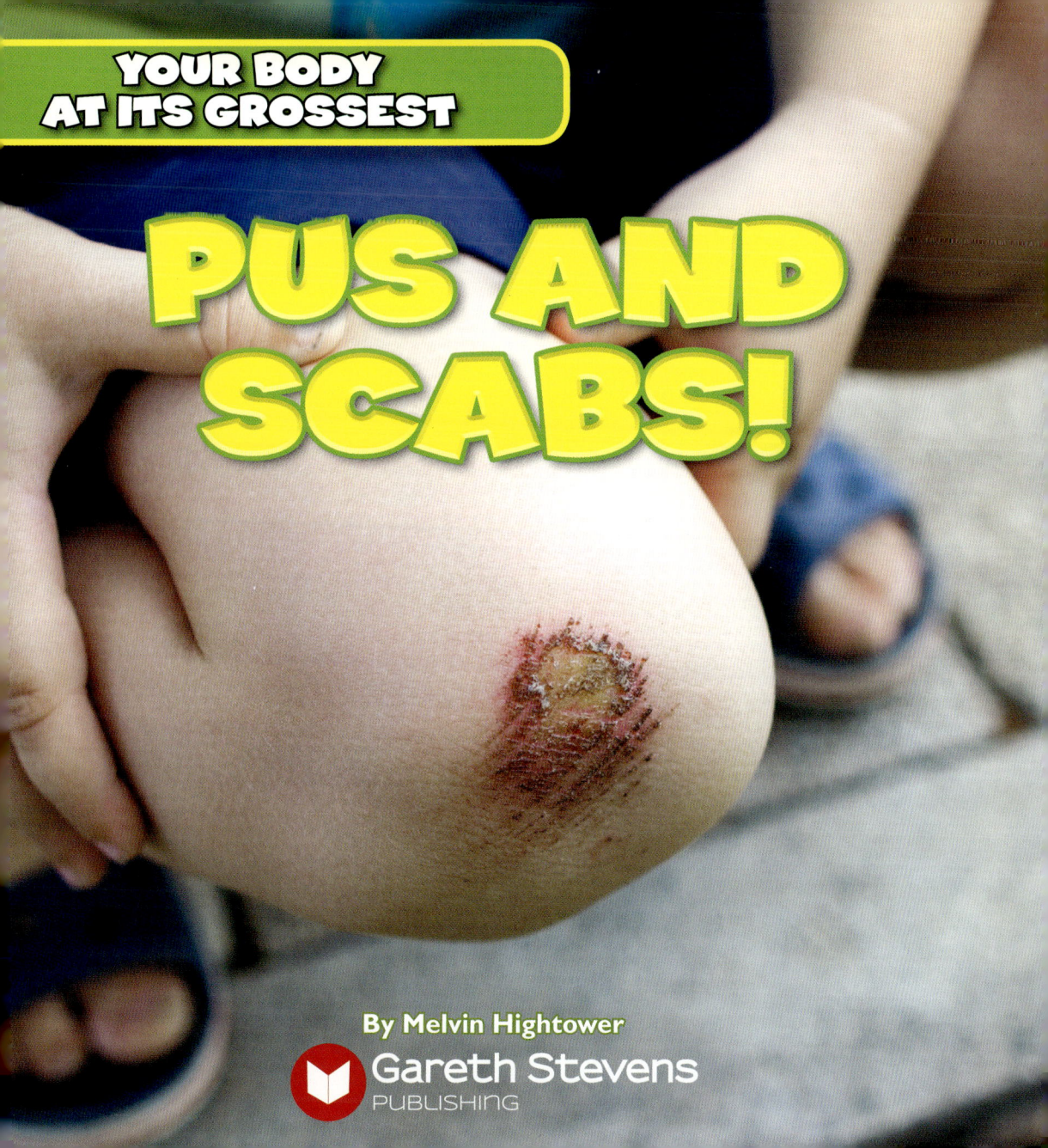

PUS AND SCABS!

YOUR BODY AT ITS GROSSEST

By Melvin Hightower

Gareth Stevens
PUBLISHING

Please visit our website, www.garethstevens.com. For a free color catalog of all our high-quality books, call toll free 1-800-542-2595 or fax 1-877-542-2596.

Cataloging-in-Publication Data

Names: Hightower, Melvin.
Title: Pus and scabs! / Melvin Hightower.
Description: New York : Gareth Stevens Publishing, 2018. | Series: Your body at its grossest | Includes index.
Identifiers: ISBN 9781482464696 (pbk.) | ISBN 9781482464931 (library bound) | ISBN 9781482464702 (6 pack)
Subjects: LCSH: Wound healing–Juvenile literature. | Wounds and injuries–Juvenile literature.
Classification: LCC RD93.H54 2018 | DDC 617.1–dc23

Published in 2018 by
Gareth Stevens Publishing
111 East 14th Street, Suite 349
New York, NY 10003

Copyright © 2018 Gareth Stevens Publishing

Designer: Sarah Liddell
Editor: Ryan Nagelhout

Photo credits: Cover, p. 1 NChi/Shutterstock.com; background gradient used throughout rubikscubefreak/Shutterstock.com; background bubbles used throughout ISebyl/Shutterstock.com; p. 5 tobkatrina/Shutterstock.com; pp. 7, 17 gritsalak karalak/Shutterstock.com; p. 9 Sebastian Kaulitzki/Shutterstock.com; p. 11 Ljupco Smokovski/Shutterstock.com; p. 13 Designua/Shutterstock.com; p. 15 Doidam/Shutterstock.com; p. 19 studio on line/Shutterstock.com; p. 21 Phatthanit/Shutterstock.com.

All rights reserved. No part of this book may be reproduced in any form without permission in writing from the publisher, except by a reviewer.

Printed in China

CPSIA compliance information: Batch #CS17GS: For further information contact Gareth Stevens, New York, New York at 1-800-542-2595.

CONTENTS

Ouch! 4
Cut Too Deep. 6
Send Help! 8
Make a Clot. 10
Keep It Together 12
Crusty Scabs 14
Working Under It All 16
Fight the Pus 18
Don't Pick It! 20
Glossary. 22
For More Information 23
Index 24

Boldface words appear in the glossary.

Ouch!

It's never fun to get a cut. You might start to bleed. It also hurts a lot! While your cut heals, or mends, you might see pus and scabs. But it's okay—that's your body working to make you better!

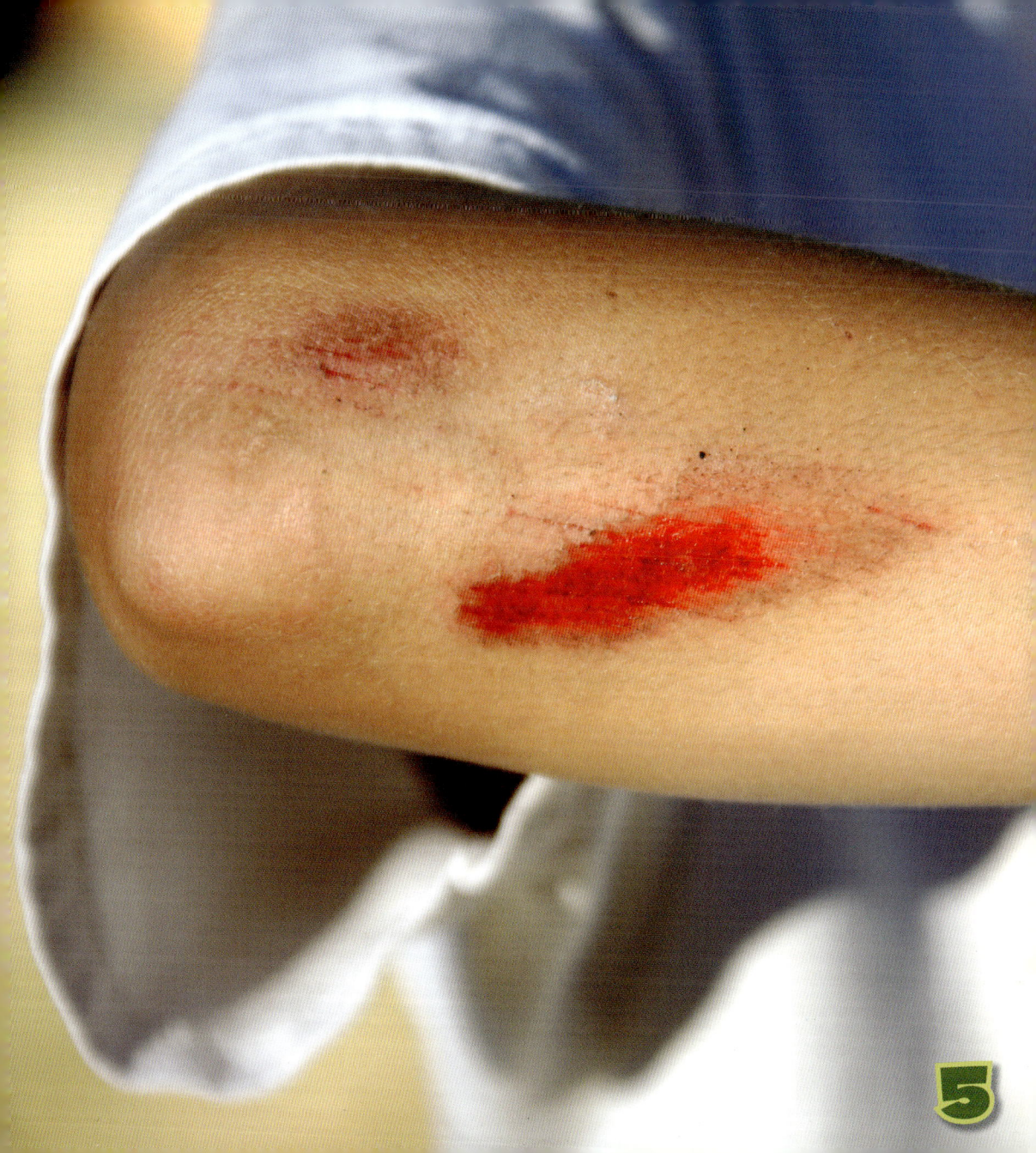

Cut Too Deep

Your skin is an amazing **organ**. It's the first line of **defense** in your **immune system**. It's made of many **layers** that work to keep you safe. When you get a cut deep in your skin, it opens a **blood vessel**, and you bleed.

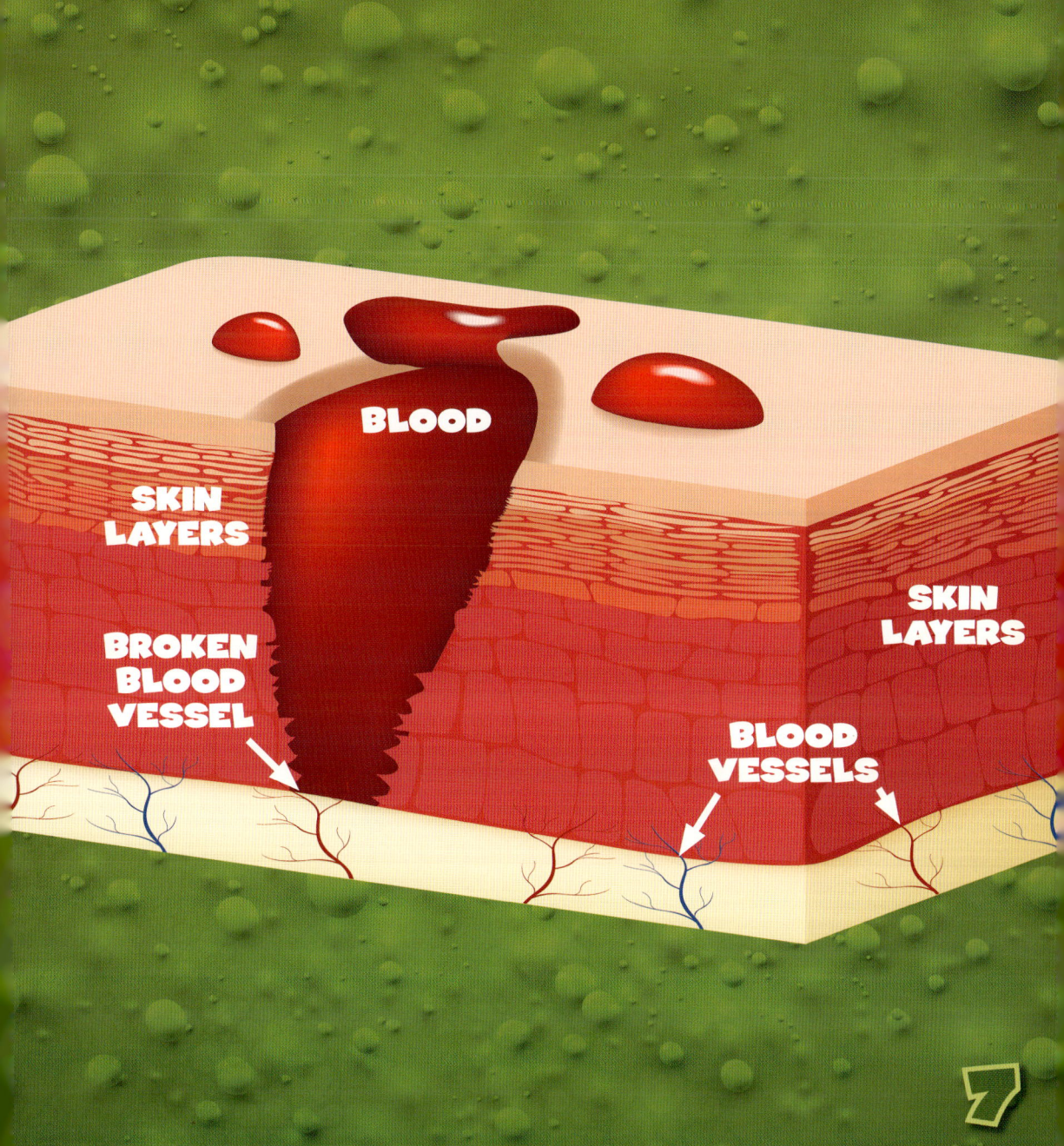

Send Help!

Blood is always moving around your body. It carries matter such as the gas oxygen, which all parts of the body need, and waste. It also has special cells called platelets. When you bleed, your body sends more platelets to the blood vessel that was cut!

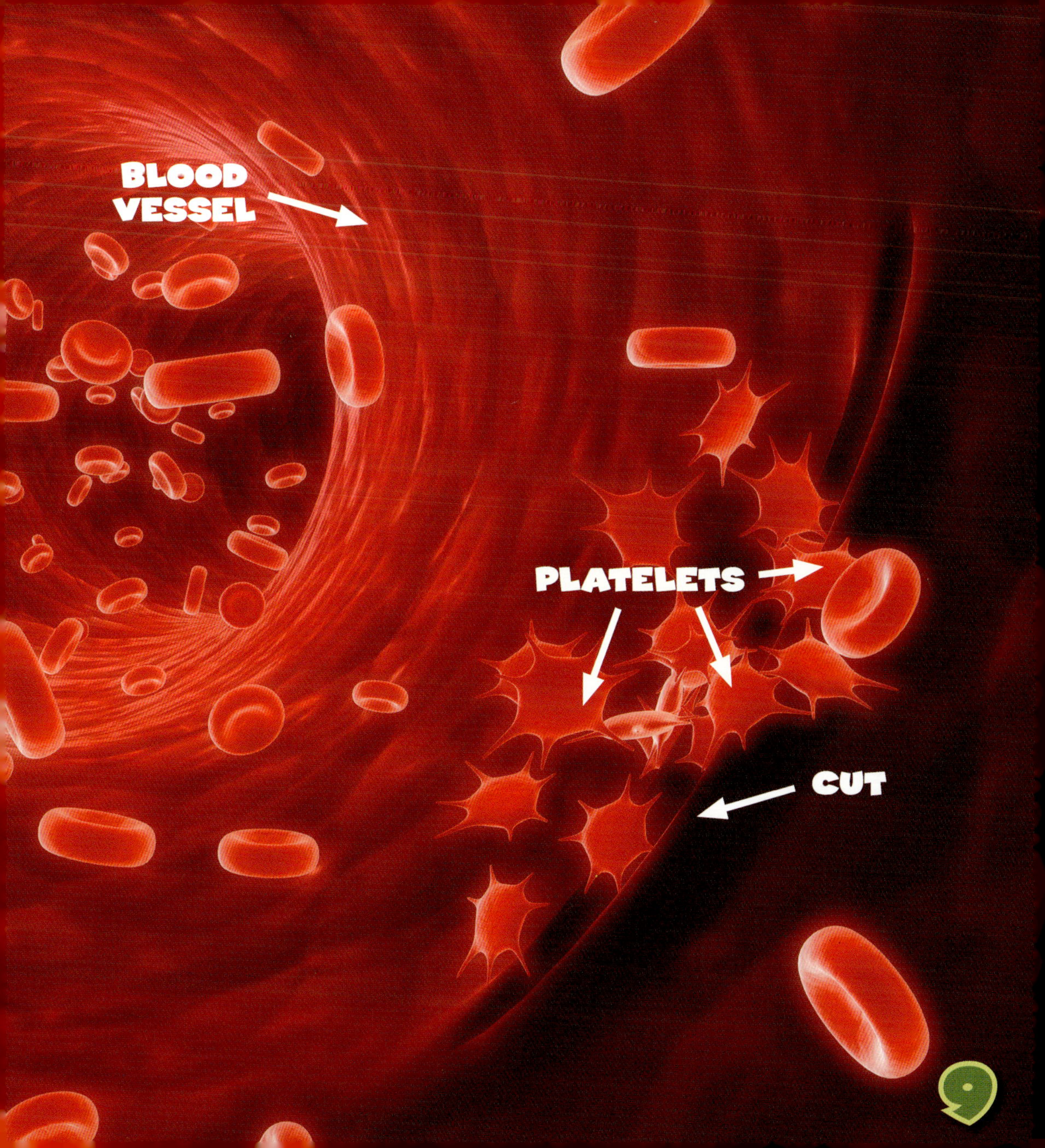
BLOOD VESSEL
PLATELETS
CUT

Make a Clot

Platelets gather together and try to help block the hole in the vessel made by the cut. This is called a blood clot. This clot stops blood from flowing out of your body. You can help blood clot!

HOW TO HELP BLOOD CLOT

- RUN COLD WATER OVER CUT
- DRY IT WITH CLOTH
- PRESS ON IT
- WEAR A BANDAGE

11

Keep It Together

Clots are full of platelets and other things to keep your cut closed. Fibrin (FY-bruhn) is threadlike stuff that holds clots together. As days go by, the clot dries out and gets hard. It makes a scab!

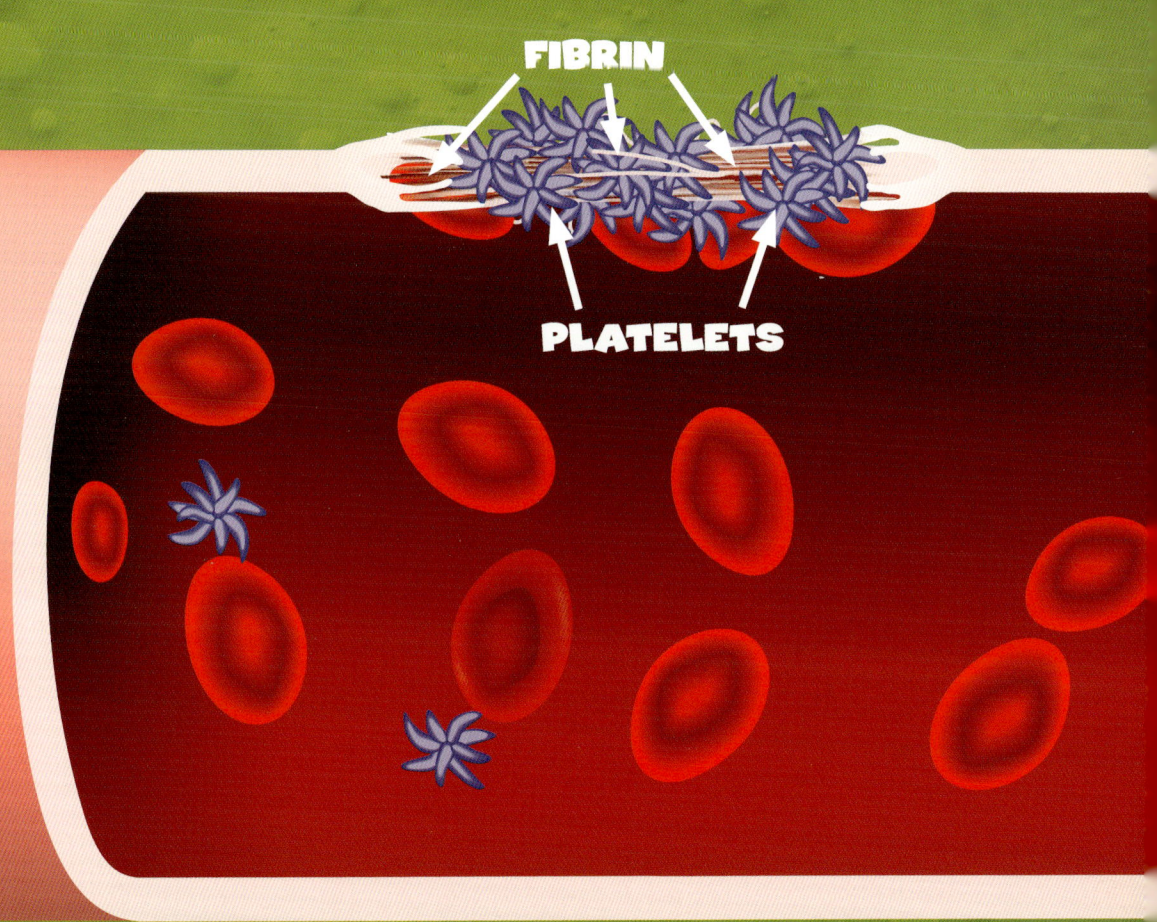

Crusty Scabs

Scabs aren't smooth on the skin. They're dry and crusty. Sometimes they're brown or red and look like dried blood. But they're important! They keep **germs** and other matter out of the cut while it heals!

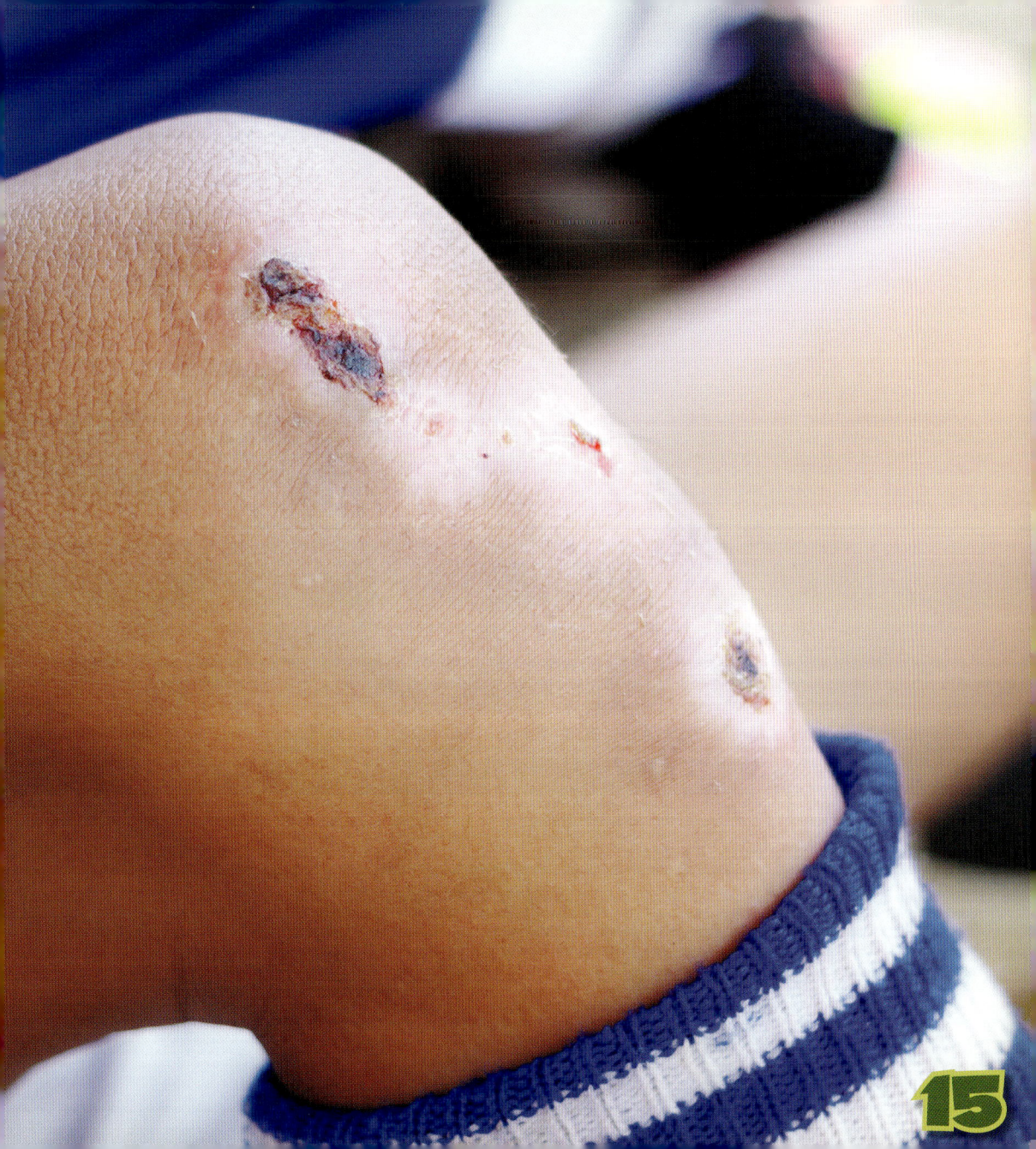

Working Under It All

While a scab covers a cut, the body works hard to fix itself. New skin cells are made to fix the layers of skin that were hurt when you were cut. Blood vessels are also fixed so you won't bleed again.

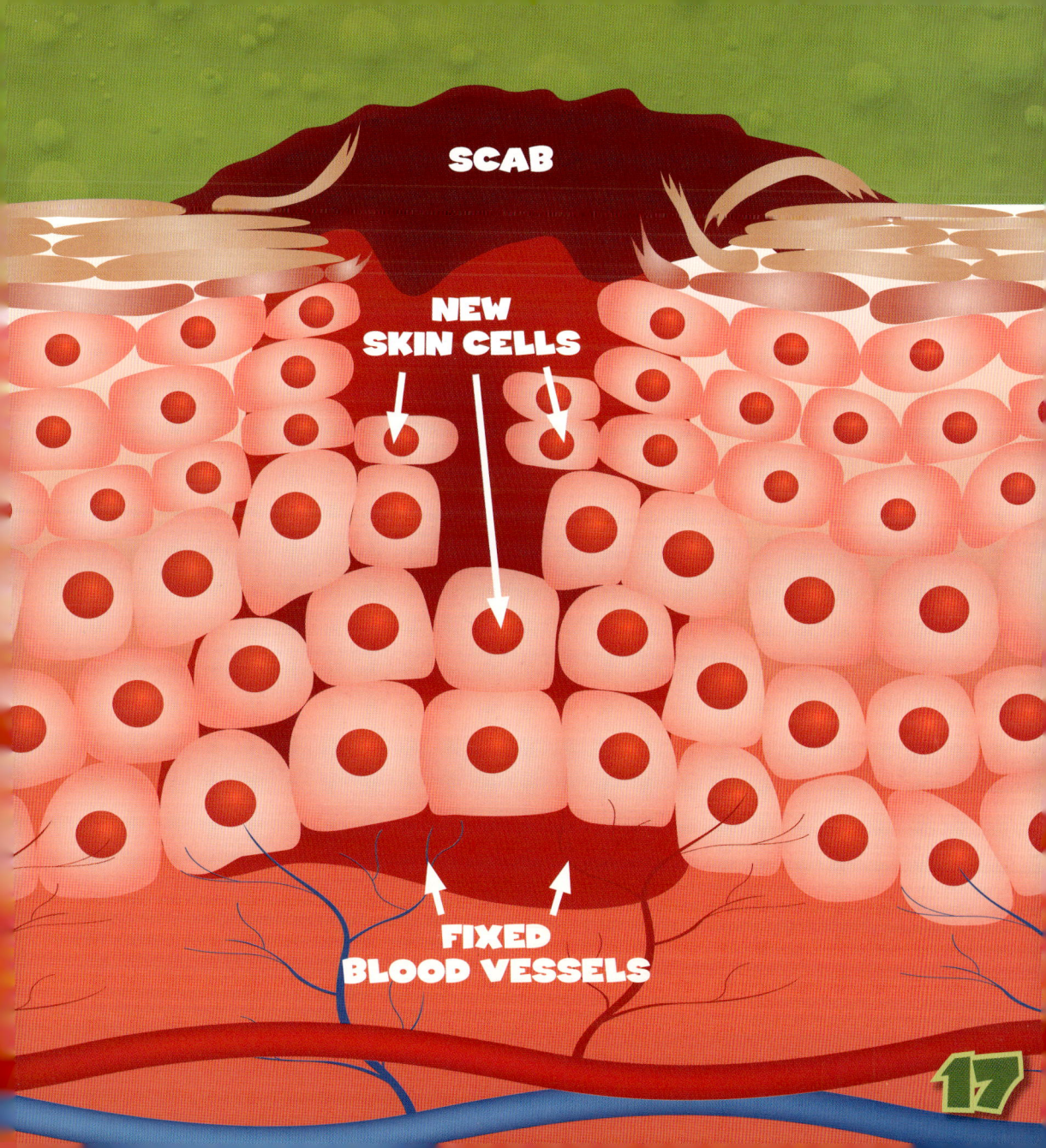

Fight the Pus

White blood cells are cells that fight **infection**. They fight germs near the cut. If it gets infected, though, you might see pus. This is white or yellowish liquid that might come out of a cut. Infected cuts need **medicine** to get better. Otherwise, you might get sick!

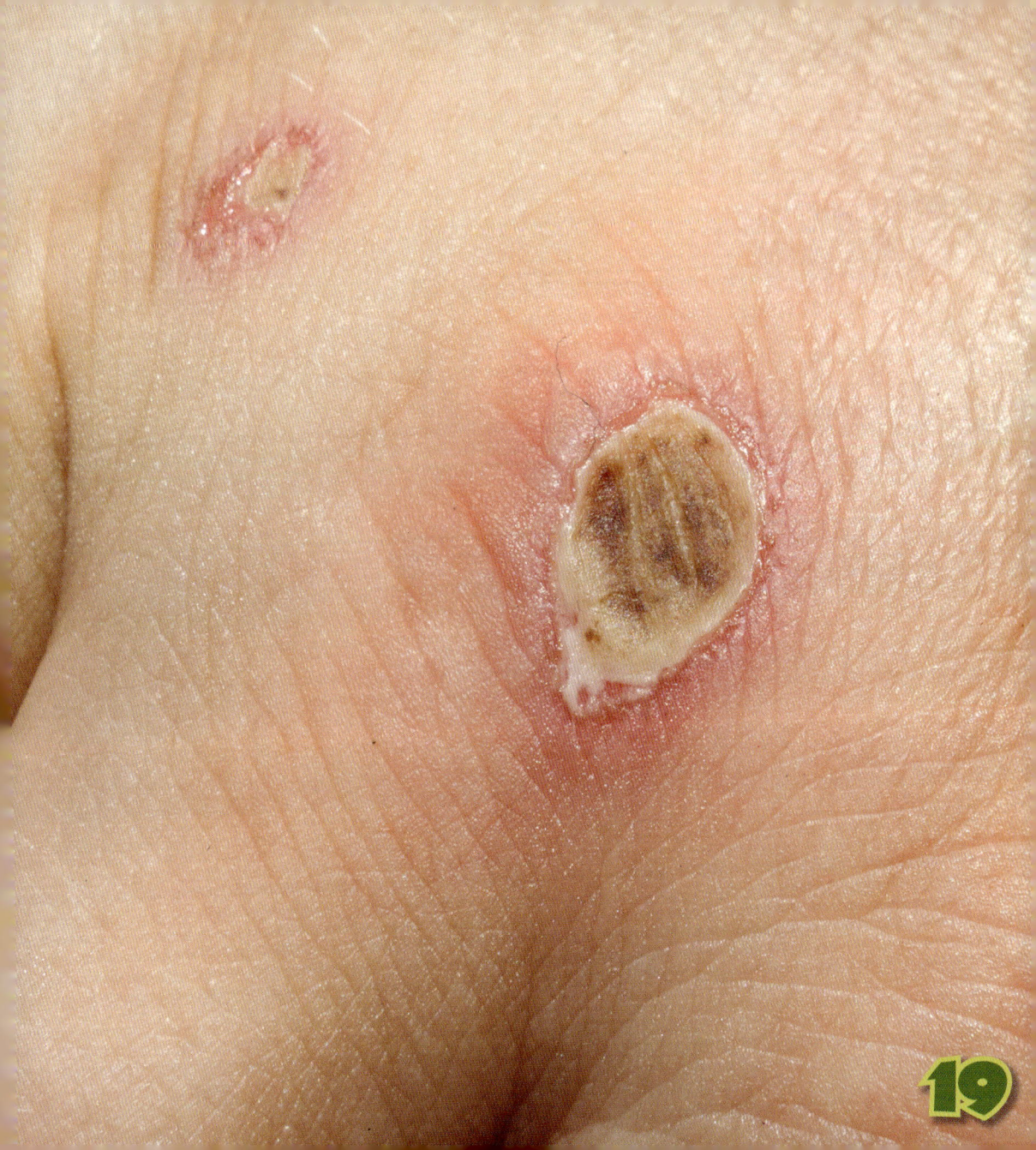

Don't Pick It!

If you have a scab, leave it alone! Scabs fall off on their own after a few weeks. It can take longer for your skin to heal if you pick at a scab. You can even get a **scar** if you cause more harm!

GLOSSARY

bandage: a piece of cloth or material used to cover a wound

blood vessel: a small tube in the body that carries blood

defense: a way of guarding against something

germ: a tiny creature that can cause sickness

immune system: the parts of the body that keep it healthy

infection: the state of being sick from the spread of germs inside the body

layer: one thickness of something lying over or under another

medicine: a drug taken to make a sick person well

organ: a part in the body that does a certain thing

scar: a mark left on the skin after it is harmed

FOR MORE INFORMATION

BOOKS

Conrad, David. *Burps, Boogers, and Other Body Functions.* Mankato, MN: Capstone Press, 2012.

Lew, Kristi. *Clot & Scab: Gross Stuff About Your Scrapes, Bumps, and Bruises.* Minneapolis, MN: Millbrook Press, 2010.

WEBSITES

The Science of Scabs
kidzworld.com/article/3181-the-science-of-scabs
Discover what makes scabs and how they work here.

What's a Scab?
kidshealth.org/en/kids/scab.html
Learn more about blood platelets and scabs here.

What's Blood?
kidshealth.org/en/kids/blood.html
Find out more about what's in blood on this site.

Publisher's note to educators and parents: Our editors have carefully reviewed these websites to ensure that they are suitable for students. Many websites change frequently, however, and we cannot guarantee that a site's future contents will continue to meet our high standards of quality and educational value. Be advised that students should be closely supervised whenever they access the Internet.

INDEX

bandage 11
blood 8, 10, 14
blood vessel 6, 8, 10, 16
cells 8, 16, 18
clot 10, 12
fibrin 12
germs 14, 18
immune system 6
infection 18
medicine 18
organ 6
platelets 8, 10, 12
pus 4, 18
scabs 4, 12, 14, 16, 20
scar 20
skin 6, 16, 20
white blood cells 18